6/07

DOES A CHIMP WEAR CLOTHES?

Fred Ehrlich, M.D.

Pictures by Emily Bolam

Blue Apple Books

Maplewood, N.J.

CIP Data is available.
Published in the United States 2005 by
Blue Apple Books
515 Valley Street, Maplewood, N.J. 07040
www.blueapplebooks.com
Distributed in the U.S. by Chronicle Books

First Edition
Printed in China
ISBN: 1-59354-122-8
1 3 5 7 9 10 8 6 4 2

Who wears clothes?
Does a chimp?

Chimps wear clothes only when they are dressed by people.

Does a donkey wear clothes?

A donkey might wear a straw hat while working in the hot sun.

But you will never see a donkey with a shirt and trousers!

Does a polar bear wear boots?

Never.
A polar bear has hairy pads on its feet
and thick fur on its legs.

It does not need boots.

Does a musk ox wear an overcoat?

A musk ox doesn't need an overcoat because it has thick fur everywhere—even on its face.

It stays warm even
when the weather is very cold.

Does a duck wear diapers?

No, silly!
Diapers are for babies.

Grown-ups put diapers on babies so they don't pee and poop all over the house.

After a while, babies grow up and learn to pee and poop in the bathroom.

Then there are no more diapers!

Only people wear clothing—
lots of different kinds.

They wear hats to protect their heads
from falling objects, from sun, and from cold.

They wear all kinds of coats to protect
their bodies from cold, wind, rain, and fire.

Animals do not need protection for their hands and feet, but people do. On their hands they wear:

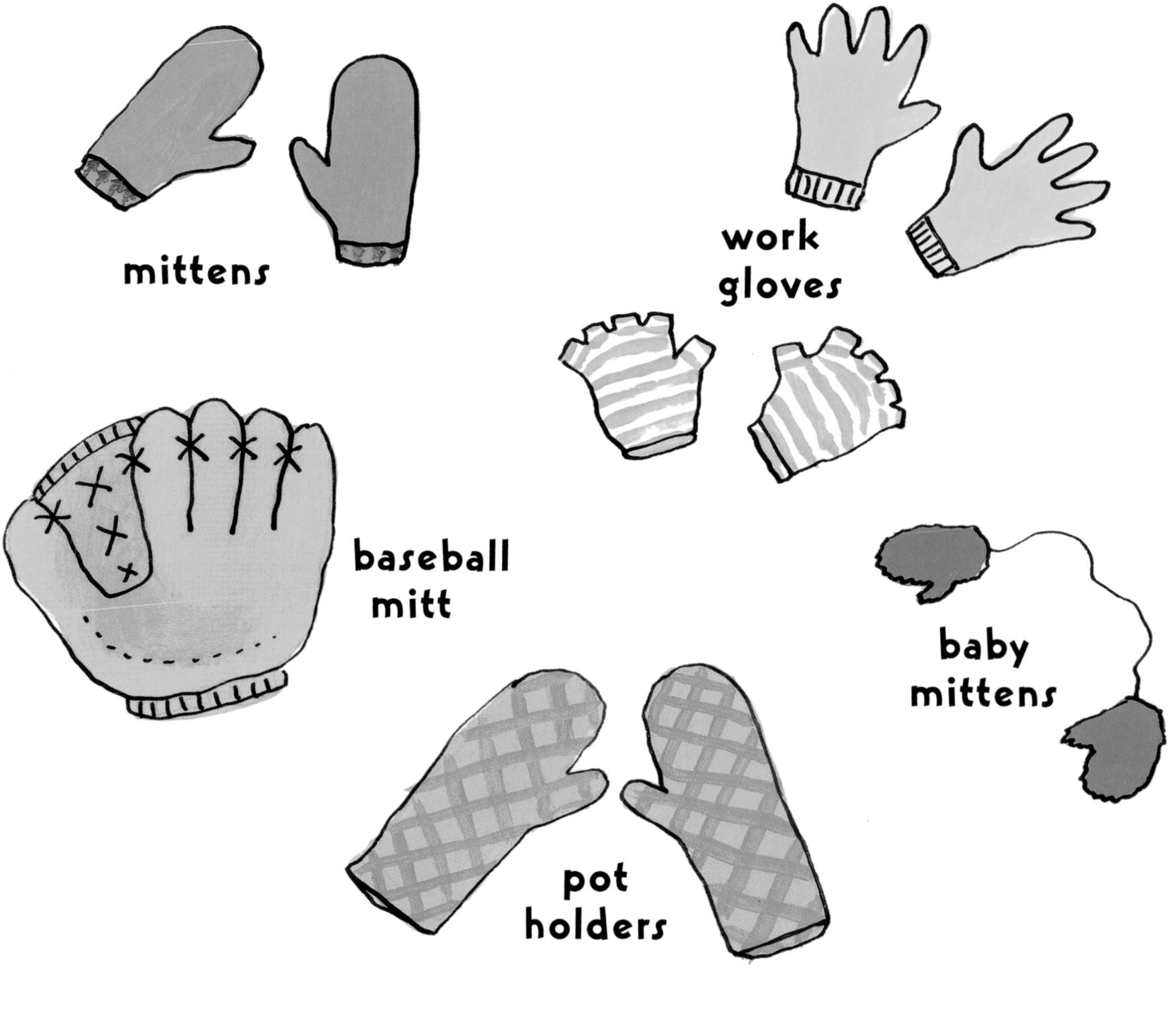

On their feet they wear:

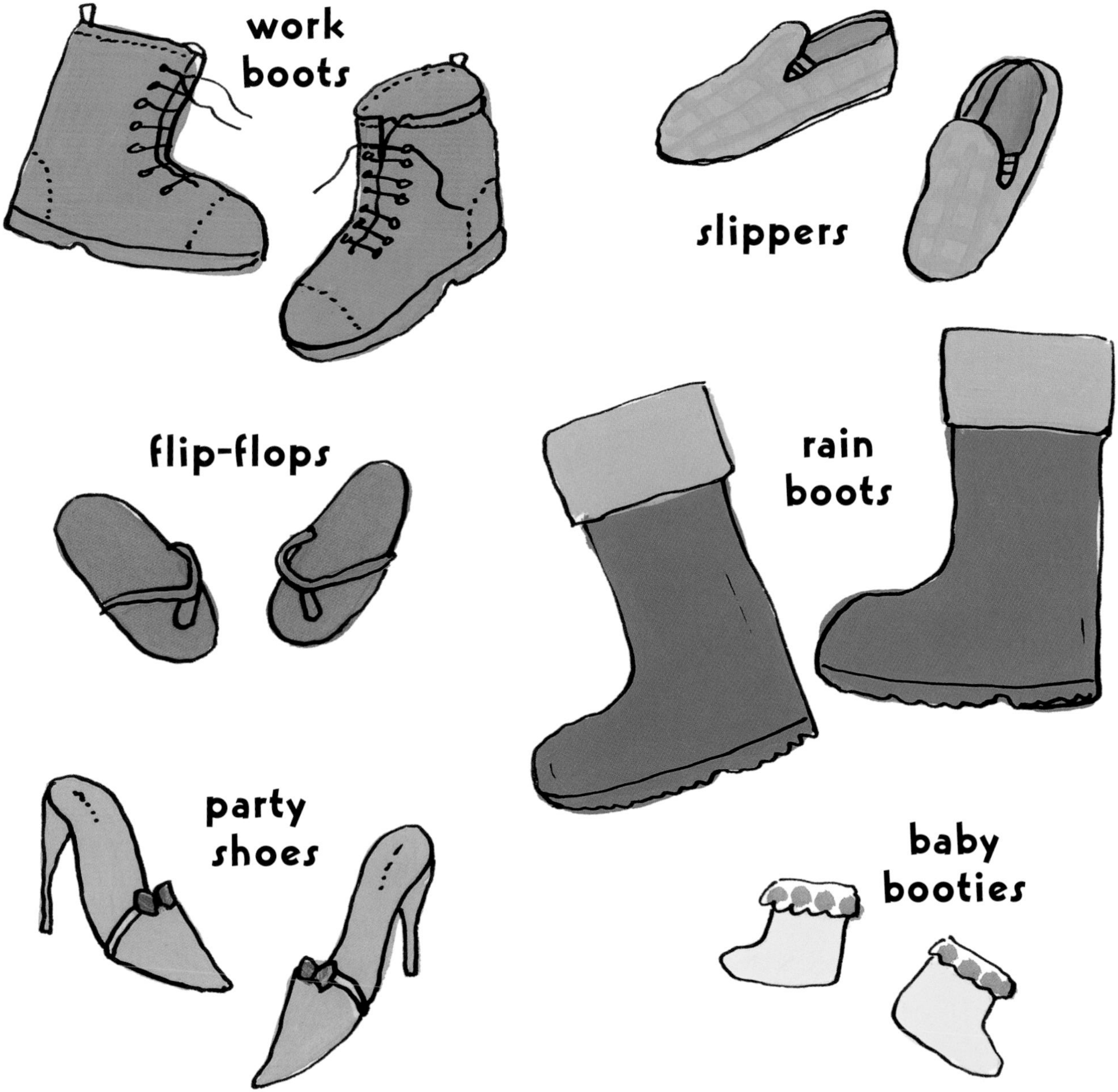

Some people put clothes on animals they take care of.

This dog is wearing a coat and a hat to keep it warm.

But a wild dog or a wild horse
would never wear clothes.

People wear all different kinds of clothing—
for work, for play, and for special occasions.

soccer player

waiter

carpenter

swimmer

diver

baseball player

underground worker

ballerina

doctor

chef

Sometimes people dress up in costumes.
Then they can pretend to be someone else.

Sometimes they dress up
for special occasions.

They wear party hats, party shoes,
party dresses, and fancy suits.

What clothing do you like to wear?